# The Child's World of
# MANNERS

NUACS- St. Anthony Elem. Bldg.
514 N. Washington St.
New Ulm, MN 56073

Copyright © 1998 by The Child's World®, Inc.
All rights reserved. No part of this book may be reproduced or
utilized in any form or by any means without written permission
from the publisher.
Printed in the U.S.A.

**Library of Congress Cataloging-in-Publication Data**
Ziegler, Sandra, 1938-
The Child's World of Manners/by Sandra Ziegler
p.   cm.
Summary: Provides suggestions for practicing good manners in
various social situations.
ISBN 1-56766-393-1 (alk. paper)
1. Etiquette for children and youth. [1. Etiquette.] I. Title.
BJ1857.C5Z53   1997
395—dc21                               96-48269
                                          CIP
                                          AC

# The Child's World of
# MANNERS

By Sandra Ziegler • Illustrated by Mechelle Ann

## THE CHILD'S WORLD®

What are good manners?

Asking your friend to come inside instead of letting her stand in the rain is good manners. And so is saying, "Let me hang up your raincoat."

When you get an invitation to a birthday party, calling to say you're coming is good manners.

When you are serving tea to a friend, and another friend arrives, showing good manners is saying, "Come in."

Showing good manners is splitting the last of the lemonade with your friend when you are both hot and thirsty from running a race.

Using your napkin to wipe messy fingers shows good manners.

Good manners is chewing with your mouth closed and not talking with your mouth full.

When you and your friend paint pictures at her house, good manners is helping to wash the brushes and put the paints away.

When you show good manners, people know you care about them and not just about yourself.

Have you used good manners today?